By Wanda Coven

Illustrated by Priscilla Burris

LITTLE SIMON
New York London Toronto Sydney New Delhi

An imprint of Simon & Schuster Children's Publishing Division
1230 Avenue of the Americas, New York, New York 10020

For information about special discounts for bulk purchases, please contact Simon & Schuster Special Sales at 1-866-506-1949 or business@simonandschuster.com.
The Simon & Schuster Speakers Bureau can bring authors to your live event. For more information or to book an event contact the Simon & Schuster Speakers Bureau at 1-866-248-3049 or visit our website at www.simonspeakers.com.
Designed by Laura Lyn DiSiena
Manufactured in the United States of America 0217 MTN
10 9 8 7
Coven, Wanda.
Heidi Heckelbeck is ready to dance! / by Wanda Coven ; illustrated by Priscilla Burris.
p. cm.
Summary: Feeling totally untalented, Heidi resorts to her book of spells to come up with a dazzling act for the school talent show.
ISBN 978-1-4424-5191-9 (pbk. : alk. paper) —
ISBN 978-1-4424-5192-6 (hardcover : alk. paper) —
ISBN 978-1-4424-5193-3 (ebook)
[1. Talent shows—Fiction. 2. Witches—Fiction.] I. Burris, Priscilla, ill. II. Title.
PZ7.C83393Hj 2013
[Fic]—dc23
2011046288

CONTENTS

AN AWFUL TRUTH

Heidi Heckelbeck sat on the maple-tree swing and twirled the ropes together until they were tight. Then she lifted her feet and let the swing go. She spun round and round. Her thoughts were spinning as fast as the swing.

“You want to hear an awful truth?” asked Heidi as the swing unwound.

“I guess so,” said her brother, Henry, who was sitting on the branch above her.

Heidi took a deep breath.

"Okay, here goes," she said. "I have no talent.

"I can't dance.

"I can't sing.

"I can't even act.

"I'm just a big fat nothing!"

"Well, *I'm* not," Henry said. "I've got talent."

"Like what?" asked Heidi.

Henry stood on the branch. He put one hand on the trunk and the other high in the air. "I am an ac-TOR!" he said.

Heidi rolled her eyes. "A BAD actor."

"No, a MIME actor," said Henry. "I can act out stories without talking."

"No words?" Heidi asked.

"Not a one," said Henry.

"Really? This I've GOT to see," said Heidi.

"Okay," said Henry as he jumped out of the tree. "But I need a smooth floor."

Heidi and Henry ran inside. Then Henry hid behind the kitchen door.

"Ready?" asked Henry.

"Ready," said Heidi.

Henry moonwalked smoothly into

the kitchen. He had his hands in his pockets as his feet glided across the floor. He moved his head forward and back as he walked. One heel snapped to the floor in between steps. Then he stopped and looked around. His eyes got wide as he pretended to see something.

I wonder what Henry's looking at, thought Heidi.

Henry stooped and pretended to pick a flower. He pretended to smell it. Then he picked another and another. When he had a whole bunch of pretend flowers, he walked

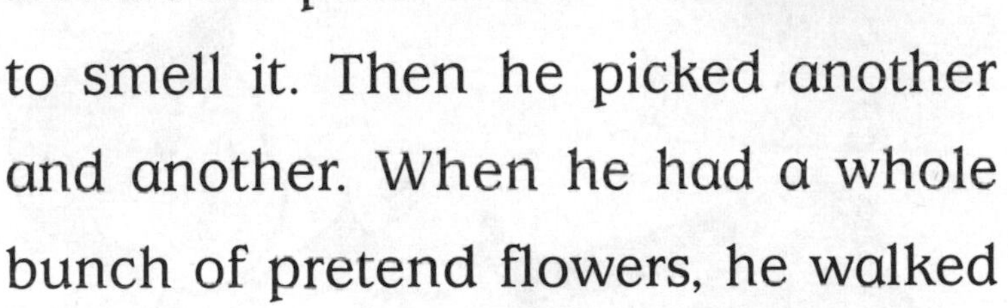

up to Heidi and offered them to her.

Heidi smiled and pretended to take them. "Very smooth, little dude," she said. "But it totally stinks."

"Why?" asked Henry.

"Because *you've* got talent and you're *younger* than I am."

"That's so silly," Henry said.

"I have to agree," said Mom, who had walked in during the show. "Everyone has talent. You just have to find something you like to do and practice it."

"But how am I going to do that?" asked Heidi. "There's only one week until the school talent show. That's not enough time to get good at anything."

"You can say that again," said Henry. "I've been practicing my mime act for months."

"See?" Heidi said. "It takes a *long* time to get good at something."

Mom sighed.

"You don't need more time or more talent," said Mom. "All you need is a good idea."

"Okay, fine," said Heidi. "I'm going outside to think."

Heidi pushed on the screen door, and it snapped shut behind her.

Just then Dad walked into the kitchen. "Did I miss something?" he asked.

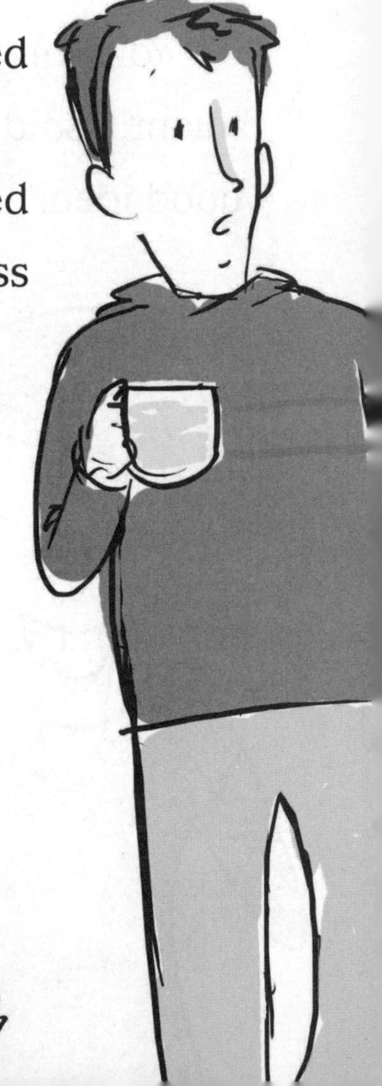

Heidi leaned against the maple tree and folded her arms. *How come Henry got all the talent in our family?* she wondered. *It's not fair.* Then Heidi spied a fat stick on the ground. She picked it up and poked at a knot in the tree. She hardly heard the back door

swing shut. Mom, Dad, and Henry had walked out into the yard.

"I've got something to cheer you up," said Mom. She set a tray of peanut butter cookies and a pitcher of milk on the picnic table.

Heidi continued to jab at the knot in the tree. It sounded hollow inside.

Maybe a squirrel lives in there, she thought. She stopped poking the tree. Heidi wished she could live inside a tree. *Then I wouldn't have to worry about being in a dumb talent show.*

"The cookies are still warm," said Dad, trying to get Heidi to the picnic table.

"And if you don't get over here, I'm going to eat yours all up," said Henry.

Heidi threw her stick on the ground. "Hey!" she barked. "Stay away from my cookies!"

"Oooh, I'm so scared," Henry said.

Heidi marched over to the picnic table, grabbed a cookie, and took a great big bite. *Mmmm,* she thought.

The warm, peanut-buttery goodness made her feel a teeny bit better.

"Maybe we can help you come up with an idea for the talent show," said Mom.

"Great idea!" said Dad. "Why don't you tell jokes? You're *very* funny."

"Too risky," Heidi said. "I might get booed off the stage."

"You could hula-hoop," said Mom.

"I can only do three twirls," said Heidi.

"Ride a unicycle!" Henry said.

"Too weird," said Heidi.

Heidi's family had more ideas—baton twirling, magic tricks, a puppet show, and reading poetry. But Heidi had an excuse for everything.

"What are Lucy and Bruce doing?" asked Mom.

"A skit," said Heidi. "They asked me to join them, but I didn't want to."

"Why?" asked Henry.

"Because I'm not into acting," said Heidi. "Especially after I had to play the role of a scary apple tree in *The Wizard of Oz*."

"So you'd rather give up than try one of our cool ideas?" asked Henry.

"Pretty much," said Heidi.

A SHOW-STOPPER

Bruce Bickerson set down his lunch tray and sat next to Heidi.

"So?" he said.

"So, *what*?" asked Heidi.

"So, did you come up with an idea for the talent show?" asked Bruce.

Heidi dropped her carrot into her

lunch bag. Before she could answer, Melanie Maplethorpe, who never said anything nice to Heidi, answered for her.

"Didn't you hear?" said Melanie in a sugary-sweet voice. "Heidi can't be in the show because she's a weirdo with no talent."

Heidi looked at her peanut butter sandwich. Her cheeks began to burn.

"Very funny, Melanie," said Lucy Lancaster. "And I'll bet you have a showstopping number planned for the talent show?"

"Of course," Melanie said. "I'm going to perform an Irish step dance

that I made up myself. I've been taking lessons at the All-Star Dance Academy for four years. I'm pretty amazing."

Lucy rolled her eyes.

Bruce's mouth fell open.

Heidi stared at her sandwich.

"Well, see you around," Melanie said. She did her famous twirl and

walked off with Stanley Stonewrecker. Poor Stanley had to carry Melanie's lunch tray. He smiled weakly at Heidi, but she never looked up from her sandwich.

"Don't let Melanie bug you, Heidi," said Lucy. "The only thing SHE is good at is being mean."

But Melanie *did* bug Heidi. She made Heidi feel like the biggest weirdo on earth.

"I have an idea," Bruce said. "Maybe you could imitate Melanie for the talent show."

"You mean pretend to be Melanie onstage?" asked Heidi.

"Exactly," Bruce said.

Heidi smiled. "Been there, done that."

"Oh yeah!" said Bruce. "You were Melanie for Halloween!"

"How could we forget?" said Lucy.

"Well, I guess you can't do that again."

"Are you sure you don't want to do a skit with us?" asked Bruce.

"I'm sure," Heidi said with a sigh.

But Heidi wasn't sure about anything. Meanie Melanie's words had made Heidi feel worse than ever. Now she had to perform in the talent show just to prove she wasn't a weirdo—even though she felt like one. But what could she do?

MAYBE? MAYBE NOT!

"Boys and girls!" said Mr. Doodlebee, the art teacher. "Today I want you to paint a picture of your house. Add as many details as you can."

This sounds like fun, thought Heidi. *Maybe my talent is art.* Heidi painted her house frog green with crisscross shingles on the roof. Then she dabbed rosebushes with pink buds on either side of the front door.

Heidi liked her picture until she saw Natalie Newman's. Natalie's house had shutters and window boxes. She had even painted a porch with rocking chairs, a flag, and a dog. *Wow,* thought Heidi. *Natalie's picture should be in a museum.*

Then Heidi looked back at her own picture. Suddenly it looked like a two-year-old had painted it. She tossed it aside. *Looks like I have zero*

talent in art, she thought. *But who knows? Maybe I can do something sporty in the talent show. . . .*

Heidi decided to try her hardest in gym class. Everyone went outside and the teacher split the class into two teams for kickball. Heidi was up first. *I'm a good kicker,* she thought as she waited for the ball.

Stanley rolled the ball to Heidi. She kicked as hard as she could, but she missed and landed smack on her bottom. Melanie laughed in the outfield.

Heidi got up and tried again. This time Heidi kicked the ball good and hard. The only trouble was that Stanley caught it!

"Out!" shouted Melanie.

Heidi walked to the end of the line.

Charlie Chen was up next. He kicked the ball over the fence and into the woods. It was an automatic home run. He ran the bases and high-fived Heidi and some of their other teammates.

Heidi sighed. *Looks like I stink at sports, too,* she thought.

In music, the class had solo tryouts for the winter concert. Heidi loved the theme: The Songs of Broadway.

"Are you trying out?" asked Lucy.

"I dunno," Heidi said. "Are you?"

"Definitely," said Lucy.

Heidi twirled her hair. *Maybe I should try out,* she thought. *Maybe my talent is singing. But what if my voice sounds funny? What if I throw up?*

Heidi's palms felt so sweaty just thinking about it.

She decided to watch some of her classmates try out first. Lucy walked to the front of the class and sang a song from *Annie*.

"Very good!" said Mr. Jacobs, the music teacher, as Lucy took her seat.

Eve Etsy went next.

"I'm going to sing 'My Favorite Things' from *The Sound of Music*,"

said Eve. When she finished singing, everyone clapped and whistled.

"Well done, Eve," said Mr. Jacobs. "You have perfect pitch!"

"Eve should be on Broadway," whispered Lucy.

Heidi nodded and slumped down in her chair.

After listening to Eve, Heidi decided not to try out for a solo. *Melanie's right. I have no talent,* she thought.

RISKY BUSINESS

Heidi stopped at Aunt Trudy's on the way home from school.

Aunt Trudy was mixing some rosewater perfume for her mail-order business. "What's wrong?" she asked.

"Melanie said I have no talent."

"Do you believe her?" Aunt Trudy

asked while opening a bottle.

"Yes."

"But what does Melanie know about your talents?"

"Nothing," said Heidi. "But *I* know I don't have any talents."

"Of course you do."

"Name one."

"You're a good sister to Henry," said Aunt Trudy.

"Am not. I'm mean to him all the time. Next."

"You're a great baker," Aunt Trudy said. "What about those wonderful cookies you made for your school's cookie contest?"

"They were kind of a disaster."

"Oh . . . I had forgotten. Well, your cookies might have won if you had left out the cheese."

"Next," said Heidi.

"You're a fast runner."

"True. But what am I supposed to do with that? Run across the stage for my talent show act?"

Aunt Trudy laughed. "Heidi, you're impossible," she said.

"I know."

"Listen," said Aunt Trudy, "don't be so hard on yourself. I had no idea what my talents were when I was your age, but I figured it out in time. Besides, I'm pretty sure you have stage fright—and not a lack of talent."

"I think I have both," said Heidi. "How can I go onstage if there is a chance I might look stupid?"

"It's a risk you have to take."

"Ugh," said Heidi. But she knew Aunt Trudy was right. Heidi hugged her aunt and walked down the front steps.

"You'll come up with something," said Aunt Trudy. "You always do."

"I know," said Heidi. "But what?"

TAP SHOES

Ka-thunk! Heidi heard a loud thump as she walked in the front door. *Whump!*

There it goes again, thought Heidi. The noise sounded like it was coming from the attic. Heidi closed the front door and ran up the stairs. Then she crept to the attic door and pulled it open.

"Hello?" she called into the rafters.

"Heidi? Is that you?" asked Dad.

"Yes, it's me," Heidi said as she ran up the stairs two by two. "What are you doing up here?"

"Looking for an old science book," said Dad. "It has a

formula for wax-bottle soda candy."

"What's that?" asked Heidi.

"It's liquid candy inside a mini soda bottle that's made out of wax. You bite off the top of the bottle and drink the candy syrup inside. I used to love them as a kid. Now I want to give them a jazzy new makeover."

"Sounds cool," said Heidi.

"It is," Dad said as he pulled a pair of black patent leather shoes from a box. He laughed.

"What are those?" asked Heidi.

"They're Mom's old tap-dancing shoes. Did you know she used to be a terrific tap dancer?"

"Really?"

"Miss Clickety Toes." Dad chuckled. He put the shoes in an empty shoe box lined with crinkly paper and handed them to Heidi.

Then Dad began to dig through another box.

Heidi stared at the shoes. They

looked just about her size. She turned them over. They had metal taps on the toes and heels.

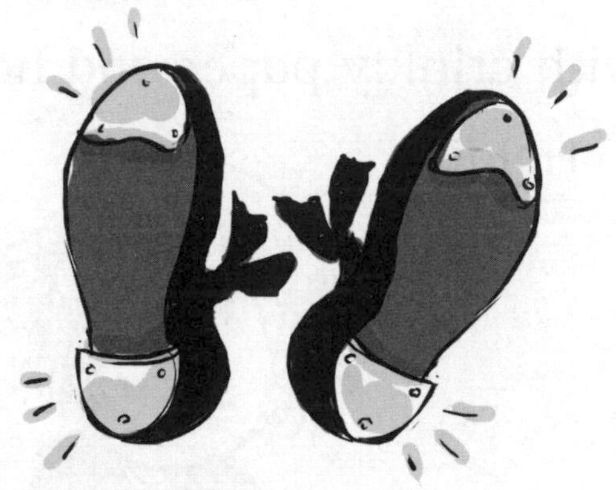

"Wow," said Heidi.

"She sure had talent," said Dad. "And so do you!"

"No, not me," Heidi said. "I'm not good at anything."

"All you would need is a few lessons."

"I don't think so."

"What about mixing?" asked Dad. "You're great at mixing. We could mix up a tornado in an empty bottle."

"No, thanks. I need to find something that I'M good at."

"But you *are* good at science experiments. I would just be giving you a little help."

"Nah," said Heidi.

Then Dad pulled a dusty book from another box. It had a cracked leather cover with gold lettering. "Aha!" he said. He blew some dust from the cover. "Here's the book I've been looking for!" Dad hugged the book to his chest.

Then he looked at Heidi. "You should think about doing a science experiment for the talent show. It's okay to get a little help sometimes."

As Dad headed for the stairs, Heidi covered the tap shoes with the lid of the box and snuck them to her room.

Hmm . . . , she thought. *Maybe Dad's right—maybe all I need is a little help.* A smile spread across her face. . . .

THE BRAVERY BUG

Heidi sat on her footstool and pulled off her sneakers. Then she wiggled her feet into her mother's tap shoes. They fit perfectly!

Heidi stepped in front of the mirror and tapped her toe on the hardwood floor. *Click!*

Then she tapped her heel. *Clack! Click! Clack!*

This could be fun, thought Heidi. She raced to her bed and pulled her *Book of Spells* out from underneath it. She looked up "dance" and found ballet, ballroom, jazz, swing, and . . .

"Tap!" said Heidi out loud. She flipped to a spell called A Classic Tap Routine and read the directions.

A Classic Tap Routine

Do you have happy feet? Are you the kind of witch who likes to shuffle from one place to another? Does entertainment run in your family? Then this is the spell for you!

Ingredients:

1 cup of root beer
3 tablespoons of cranberry juice
1 teaspoon of sugar

Mix the ingredients in a tall drinking cup. Hold your Witches of Westwick medallion in one hand and place your other hand over the mix. Chant the following words:

Fizzy, Fizzy Wizzy!
Jazzy, jazzy zap!
Make This Witch an
Expert—
help her learn to tap!
For a perfect routine,
drink the entire mix before
the performance. This spell
works instantly and lasts
up to two hours.

"Heidi!" Dad called. "Dinner!"

Heidi shoved her *Book of Spells* back under the bed. "Coming!" she yelled.

She pulled off the tap shoes and placed them back in the box. Then she slipped on her sneakers and smiled at herself in the mirror. *I'm going to rock this talent show!*

Heidi sat down at the table. “I’m so hungry I could eat a HORSE,” she said.

“Would you settle for some turkey meatballs and spaghetti?” Dad asked.

“Yes, please!” said Heidi, holding out her plate.

Dad heaped her plate with meatballs and spaghetti.

"Wow," said Henry. "You sound happy. WHAT HAPPENED?"

"I'll tell you what happened," Heidi said as she sprinkled grated cheese on her pasta. "I finally came up with an idea for the talent show."

Henry slurped a piece of spaghetti.

"You did?" asked Mom.

"Yup," said Heidi.

"What are you going to do?" asked Henry.

Heidi thought for a moment. She didn't want to say she was doing

a dance, because they would all know that at this point it would take witchcraft to pull that off. Instead she said, "It's a surprise. You'll have to wait and see."

Henry rolled his eyes.

"This is very brave," Mom said. "Since when did you get so brave?"

"Today after school," said Heidi. "I kind of got tapped by the bravery bug."

Mom raised an eyebrow.

Heidi began to examine a meatball.

"Well, I think it's great," said Dad. "After all, we are a very talented family."

Principal's
Office

WEIRDOS CAN'T DANCE!

The next morning at school Heidi stopped by the office on the way to her classroom.

"Oh hello, Heidi," said Principal Pennypacker. "Can I help you with something?"

"Yes," said Heidi. "I would like to

enter the school talent show."

"That's wonderful," said Principal Pennypacker. "What would you like to perform?"

"A dance," said Heidi.

"Any special type of dance?"

"No. Just a dance."

"I had no idea you could dance," said the principal.

"It's a hidden talent."

"Hmm. . . . I see." Then Principal Pennypacker looked Heidi in the eye and smiled. "You're always so full of surprises," he said.

Heidi laughed nervously. She often got the feeling that Principal Pennypacker knew she was a little different. *But he has no way of*

knowing that I am a witch, right?

At the end of the day, the talent show list was up! Everyone gathered around the bulletin board in the hallway to see the list of performers.

"Heidi! You signed up for the talent show!" said Lucy. "Why didn't you say anything?"

"I wanted to surprise you," said Heidi.

"Well, I'm *not* surprised," Lucy said. "I'm SHOCKED!"

"It's no big deal," said Heidi.

"Are you kidding?" Bruce said. "A few days ago you didn't want to have anything to do with the talent show!"

"Well, I changed my mind," said Heidi. "I'm going to do a dance."

"That's great," said Lucy. "What kind of dance are you going to do?"

"It's a secret," Heidi said.

"It's really *no* secret," said Melanie. "Weirdos definitely can't dance!" Then she burst out laughing.

Heidi balled up her fists at her sides. This time she would stand up to Melanie. Somehow she felt more confident now that she'd found a tap-dancing spell.

"Laugh all you want, Melanie," said Heidi. "My dance is going to be a BIG hit."

Melanie's jaw dropped. She wasn't used to Heidi standing up to her. She and her bobbing ponytail walked off.

"I'LL show her!" said Heidi.

"That's the spirit!" said Lucy.

And they slapped each other five.

HAPPY FEET!

Heidi peeked out the window. Mom was gardening. She knew Dad was in the lab. Henry was upstairs practicing his mime act. *The coast is clear,* she thought. *Now I can make my potion.*

Heidi set a tall plastic Disney cup on the kitchen counter. Then she grabbed a bottle of root beer from the refrigerator. She poured one cup of root beer into the Disney cup. Then she pulled a cranberry juice box from the pantry shelf. Heidi added three tablespoons to the cup. Next she added the sugar and stirred everything together.

Heidi carried the potion to her bedroom and set it on her desk. *Now I need something to wear,* she thought.

Heidi searched through her closet. She chose a purple dress with sparkly swirls across the

front. After getting dressed, Heidi slipped on Mom's old tap shoes.

Heidi looked at her kitty cat clock with the moving eyes and tail. *The talent show starts in an hour,* she thought. *If the spell lasts two hours, this would be the perfect time to cast the spell!*

Heidi grabbed her *Book of Spells* and put on her Witches of Westwick medallion. She held her medallion in one hand and placed her other hand over the mix. She had just begun to chant the spell when . . .

Rap! Rap! Rap!

Somebody knocked on her door! Heidi jumped to her feet and bumped

into her desk. Her potion tipped over. Heidi caught it with her free hand, but some of it sloshed onto her desk.

"Who is it?" asked Heidi. She quickly lay her jean jacket over her *Book of Spells* and medallion.

"It's Mom. We're leaving in fifteen minutes. Are you ready?"

"Almost!" said Heidi.

She listened to her mom's footsteps as she walked down the hall. *Phew!* she thought. *That was close!*

Heidi looked at the spill on her desk. Then she looked at the liquid in the cup. There was still a lot left. *This will have to do,* she thought. There wasn't enough time to sneak downstairs and make another batch.

Heidi chanted the spell and then chugged the mix. She scrunched up her face. *Yuck,* she thought. *That tastes gross.* Heidi wiped her mouth with the back of her hand and walked to the mirror to test the spell.

She tapped her toe on the floor. Her feet went *tappity-tap!* It was if they had been doing it her whole life. Heidi had to jump onto the rug to stop herself from dancing. *Wow,*

she thought. *This is even better than I imagined! I am not going to be a big nothing at the talent show after all. I'm going to be a STAR!*

Heidi stuffed the shoes back into the box, slipped on her sneakers, and zoomed downstairs.

"I'M READY!" she shouted.

THAT'S A WRAP!

Heidi hopped into the car and sat next to Henry. He had on ankle-length black trousers, white socks, and black loafers. On top he wore a black-and-white-striped shirt, suspenders, white gloves, and a black top hat. Mom had painted his face pure white with red lips.

"You look like a REAL mime," said Heidi.

Henry gave the okay signal with his fingers. He was already in character.

"Are you all set with your dance?" asked Dad.

"I haven't seen you practice once all week," said Mom. "Are you sure you're ready?"

"Yup, all set," said Heidi, giving her shoe box a little kiss.

Dad dropped Heidi and Henry off at the back of the auditorium. Kids

had gathered outside the stage door. Heidi spotted Melanie. Her hair was all curled and she had on a flouncy Irish costume with a pink bodice and four layers of pink and white ruffles.

She looked like a real dancer. Heidi tried not to notice.

Mrs. Noddywonks, the drama teacher, handed out the program to the audience. Henry's act was first!

Soon Mrs. Noddywonks announced the first performer.

"Welcome, ladies and gentlemen, to the Brewster Elementary Talent Show!" she said. "For our first act we

have Henry Heckelbeck, who will be performing a mime routine."

Everyone clapped and cheered.

Heidi gave Henry a fist bump.

Then Henry moonwalked onto the stage. *Snap! Slide! Snap! Slide!* He seemed to float across the floor. Then

he performed his flower routine. When he offered the pretend flowers to Mrs. Noddywonks, the audience roared with laughter. Henry bowed and zoomed off the stage.

"Great job!" said Heidi.

"Thanks," said Henry. "I felt a little scared."

"It didn't show," said Heidi.

The next act was Charlie Chen who played the banjo. After him Natalie Newman told jokes. Then Mrs. Noddywonks closed the curtain so that Lucy and Bruce could set up their skit.

Lucy sat on a stool in front of the curtain and put her arms behind her back. Bruce stood behind her and slipped his arms through hers.

Nobody could see Bruce because he was behind the curtain. Then Lucy began to tell a story while Bruce did all sorts of funny things to Lucy with his hands. The crowd laughed and laughed as "Lucy's hands" slapped her face and scratched her head.

Then it was Heidi's turn. She took a deep breath. Heidi walked under the lights and tapped her toe on the stage. Her feet began to shuffle. She tapped across the floor one way and then back the other way. She did digs, flaps,

and a move called the Cincinnati, which got a lot of claps and cheers.

But then . . . her feet suddenly stopped dancing! Heidi tapped the floor. Nothing happened. She tapped

again. Not one shuffle. *Oh no!* she thought. *The spell must've worn off!*

Heidi looked at the audience. People began to murmur. She tried to mimic what her feet and arms had been doing when she had been under the

spell. She could see her mom and dad in the audience. They knew she had used magic. Tears welled up in Heidi's eyes. *I'm going to be in big trouble,* she thought.

But Heidi was wrong. Her parents began to clap and whistle—and so did Aunt Trudy. The whole audience began to cheer! Heidi smiled and

quickly shuffled her way offstage.

"You were amazing!" Lucy said.

"How'd you pull that off?" asked Bruce.

"It wasn't exactly what I had planned," said Heidi, "but I'm glad everyone liked it."

"That was outstanding!" said Principal Pennypacker, who had been helping out backstage. "It was almost as if your feet had been bewitched!"

For a moment Heidi was speechless. *Does he know? But how? Nah, there's no way.* She thanked the principal and turned back to her friends.

Then Melanie pranced onto the

stage. She performed a perfect routine. Heidi wanted to barf.

"Your act was WAY better," Henry said.

Heidi spun around. "Thanks, little dude," she said. "But you know what? YOUR act stole the show."

"Really?" said Henry.

"Definitely," Heidi said.

After the last act, Heidi and Henry ran into the auditorium to find Mom, Dad, and Aunt Trudy.

Mom had a stern look on her face. Maybe her parents were a little mad after all.

"I'm sorry I used magic," said Heidi.

"That's cheating," said Mom.

"I know," said Heidi. "I just wanted to have a talent."

"Did you like tap-dancing?" asked Aunt Trudy.

"I loved it," said Heidi. "It made me want to get good at something."

"But you ARE good at something," said Henry. "You're good at getting in TROUBLE!"

Everyone laughed—even Heidi.

"I'd rather forget I have THAT talent," Heidi said.

"Bravo!" said Dad. "Now, who wants to get pizza and try out my new fizzy wax-bottle soda candy?"

"WE do!" shouted Henry and Heidi.

And they moonwalked all the way to the car.

Heidi met Lucy at the Brewster Elementary parking lot. The bus for Camp Dakota had already arrived.

"Time to go!" Heidi said.

She hugged her mom and dad good-bye.

Heidi turned to Henry. "You know what's weird?" she said. "I'm going to miss you."

"I'll miss you too," Henry said. "Write me, okay?"

An excerpt from *Heidi Heckelbeck Goes to Camp!*

“Promise,” said Heidi. She high-fived her little brother.

Then Heidi slung her backpack over her shoulder and boarded the bus with Lucy. They looked at each other and squealed.

“This is going to be the BEST two weeks EVER!” Heidi said.

“I know,” said Lucy. “And I can’t wait for you to meet my two camp friends, Jill and Bree.”

“Me too,” Heidi said.

During the ride the girls played hangman and drew pictures. Soon the bus pulled onto a dirt road lined with pine trees. A bunch of campers greeted the bus in the parking lot.

"There they are!" shouted Lucy, waving at her friends from the bus window. Heidi peeked at the girls. Both of the girls bounced up and down and waved. *Wow, they sure are happy to see Lucy,* she thought.

Heidi turned to say something to Lucy, but Lucy was already getting off the bus.

"Hey, wait for me!" shouted Heidi, bumping the seats with her backpack as she ran down the aisle.

But no one was listening to Heidi.